THIS WALKER BOOK BELONGS TO:

_____

_____

_____

_____

For Pete
C.R.

First published 1987 by Walker Books Ltd
87 Vauxhall Walk, London SE11 5HJ

This edition published 1989

Reprinted 1990
Printed in Italy by Graphicom srl

British Library Cataloguing in Publication Data
Riddell, Chris
The fibbs.
I. Title
823'.914 [J]   PZ7
ISBN 0-7445-1390-1

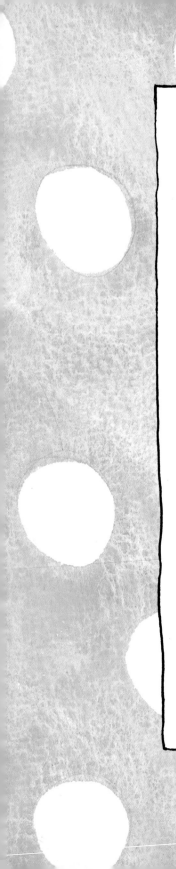

THE
FIBBS

Written and illustrated by

CHRIS RIDDELL

WALKER BOOKS
LONDON

"Did you get the bananas?" asked Mrs Fibb when Mr Fibb got back from the shops.

"Well, no," said Mr Fibb. "I meant to, but..."

"But what?" said Mrs Fibb.

"You're never going to believe this,"
said Mr Fibb, "but I had just come out of
the greengrocer's...

...when a giant hairy hand came down
from the sky and grabbed me!"

"There I was on top of an office block
in the clutches of a giant gorilla.
I could see police cars and fire engines
down below, and a huge crowd gathered.
Then from out of the clouds came fighter
planes with their guns blazing and
the gorilla got very angry."

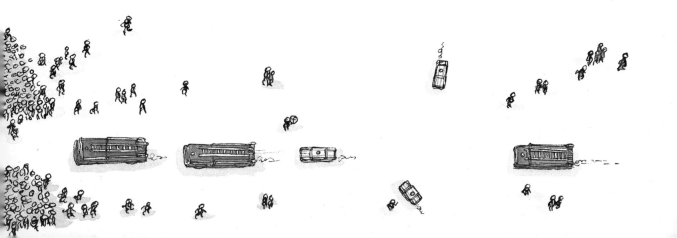

"So before there was a nasty accident
I decided to sort things out myself.
"'Excuse me,' I said to the gorilla,
'would you care for a banana?'"

"'How kind,' said the gorilla and ate
all the bananas in one mouthful."

"Then he gave me a lift home on his back.
Still, never mind, we can have
some of your chocolate cake instead."

"Well, no," said Mrs Fibb. "I was
baking today, but..."

"But what?" said Mr Fibb.

"You're never going to believe this," said Mrs Fibb, "but just after you left, something that looked like a giant tea saucer landed in the back garden. And three little green people climbed out of it and came into the kitchen.

"'We come in peace, earth woman,' they said. 'What's cooking?'

"'Nothing yet,' I said, 'but I'm about to bake a chocolate cake.'"

"'Then we shall help you,' they said and straightaway they began.

"They mixed up flour

and baked beans

and washing-up liquid

and pepper and
put it in the oven."

"Before you could say 'little green Martians' the oven door opened and a big spongy blob jumped out and started chasing the cat."

"'That's the best cake we've ever baked,' said the little green people. 'You can keep it if you like.'

"'No, thank you,' I said. 'I like earth cooking much better.'

"So then I baked them a big chocolate cake. When they had all tasted a piece, they said, 'You must give us the recipe, earth woman.'

"'Only if you take that nasty blob with you when you go,' I replied."

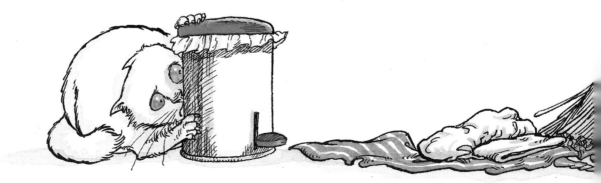

"So they did. And they took the rest
of the chocolate cake, I'm afraid.
Still, never mind, at least we can
have a cup of tea. Now where's the teapot?"

"You're never going to believe this,"
said Tommy Fibb, running into
the room, "but..."

"But what?" said Mr and Mrs Fibb.

"Well," said Tommy Fibb, "Mrs McBean from next door accidentally kicked her football through the window this morning...

...and it landed on the table
and smashed the teapot.
I meant to tell you earlier, but..."

"You can't believe a word that child says," said Mrs Fibb.

"I don't know where he gets it from,"
said Mr Fibb.

MORE WALKER PAPERBACKS

THE PRE-SCHOOL YEARS

John Satchwell
& Katy Sleight
Monster Maths
ODD ONE OUT   BIG AND LITTLE
COUNTING   SHAPES   ADD ONE   SORTING
WHAT TIME IS IT?   TAKE AWAY ONE

FOR THE VERY YOUNG

John Burningham
Concept books
COLOURS   ALPHABET
OPPOSITES   NUMBERS

Byron Barton
TRAINS   TRUCKS   BOATS   AEROPLANES

PICTURE BOOKS
For All Ages

Colin McNaughton
THERE'S AN AWFUL LOT OF WEIRDOS IN
OUR NEIGHBOURHOOD
SANTA CLAUS IS SUPERMAN

Russell Hoban
& Colin McNaughton
The Hungry Three
THEY CAME FROM AARGH!
THE GREAT FRUIT GUM ROBBERY

Jill Murphy
FIVE MINUTES' PEACE
ALL IN ONE PIECE

Bob Graham
THE RED WOOLLEN BLANKET
HAS ANYONE HERE SEEN WILLIAM?

Philippa Pearce
& John Lawrence
EMILY'S OWN ELEPHANT

David Lloyd
& Charlotte Voake
THE RIDICULOUS STORY OF
GAMMER GURTON'S NEEDLE

Nicola Bayley
Copycats
SPIDER CAT   PARROT CAT   CRAB CAT
POLAR BEAR CAT   ELEPHANT CAT

Peter Dallas-Smith
& Peter Cross
TROUBLE FOR TRUMPETS

Philippe Dupasquier
THE GREAT ESCAPE

Sally Scott
THE THREE WONDERFUL BEGGARS

Bamber Gascoigne
& Joseph Wright
AMAZING FACTS BOOKS 1 & 2

Martin Handford
WHERE'S WALLY?
WHERE'S WALLY NOW?